Monster in the Hood

Steve Antony

OXFORD
UNIVERSITY PRESS

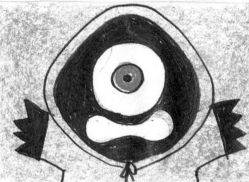

BEWARE
THE MONSTER IN THE HOOD

Sammy Squirrel, Henri Hedgehog,
and Marvin Mouse had heard all
about the **MONSTER IN THE HOOD**.

But they wanted to see it with their very own eyes . . .

. . . so Sammy Squirrel shouted,

'COME OUT, COME OUT,
WHEREVER YOU ARE!
YOU WON'T SCARE US!'

And then they heard a SQUEAK.

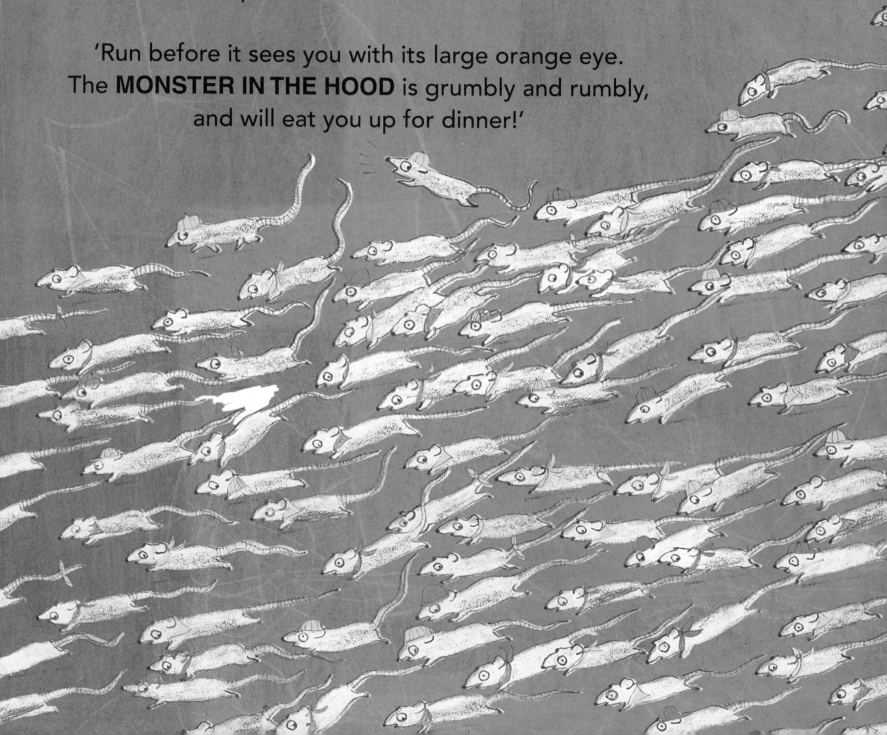

It was a pack of rats!

'There is a **MONSTER IN THE HOOD**,'
squeaked one of the rats.

'Run before it sees you with its large orange eye.
The **MONSTER IN THE HOOD** is grumbly and rumbly,
and will eat you up for dinner!'

But this didn't scare the intrepid trio . . .

. . . so Henri Hedgehog shouted,

'COME OUT, COME OUT,
WHEREVER YOU ARE!
YOU MIGHT SCARE A PACK OF RATS,
BUT YOU WON'T SCARE US!'

And then they heard a **SCREECH.**

It was a cloud of bats!

'There is a **MONSTER IN THE HOOD,**'
screeched one of the bats.

'Run before it grabs you with its huge shaggy hands.
The **MONSTER IN THE HOOD** is grumbly and rumbly,
and will eat you up for dinner!'

But this didn't scare the intrepid trio . . .

. . . so Marvin Mouse shouted,

'COME OUT, COME OUT,
WHEREVER YOU ARE!
YOU MIGHT SCARE A PACK OF RATS,
AND A CLOUD OF BATS,
BUT YOU WON'T SCARE US!'

And then they heard a SQUEAL.

It was a clutter of cats!

'There is a **MONSTER IN THE HOOD**,'
squealed one of the cats.

'Run before it chomps you with its big scary mouth.
The **MONSTER IN THE HOOD** is grumbly and rumbly,
and will eat you up for dinner!'

But this didn't scare the intrepid trio . . .

. . . so they all shouted together,

'COME OUT, COME OUT,
WHEREVER YOU ARE!
YOU MIGHT SCARE A PACK OF RATS,
AND A CLOUD OF BATS,
AND A CLUTTER OF CATS,
BUT YOU WON'T SCARE US!'

And then they heard . . . NOTHING.

There it stood, the **MONSTER IN THE HOOD**.

It had a large orange eye, just like the rat said.

And huge shaggy hands, just like the bat said.

And a big scary mouth, just like the cat said.

But what it didn't have . . .

. . . was a **FRIEND.**

'The rats, bats, and cats were all wrong,' said Sammy Squirrel.

'The **MONSTER IN THE HOOD** is kind,' said Henri Hedgehog.

'He just wanted
someone to play with,'
said Marvin Mouse.

But there was
one more thing the
MONSTER IN THE HOOD
wanted that night . . .

DINNER!

To Joseph

OXFORD
UNIVERSITY PRESS

Great Clarendon Street, Oxford, OX2 6DP,
United Kingdom

Oxford University Press is a department of the University of Oxford.
It furthers the University's objective of excellence in research,
scholarship, and education by publishing worldwide. Oxford is a
registered trade mark of Oxford University Press in the UK and in
certain other countries

Database right Oxford University Press (maker)

First Edition published in 2016

British Library Cataloguing in Publication Data available

ISBN: 978-0-19-273979-7 (paperback)
ISBN: 978-0-19-273980-3 (eBook)

1 3 5 7 9 10 8 6 4 2

Printed in China

Paper used in the production of this book is a natural, recyclable
product made from wood grown in sustainable forests.
The manufacturing process conforms to the environmental
regulations of the county of origin.